JP SCH
Schatzer, Jeffery L.
The bird in Santa's beard
how a Christmas legend

I0689960

The Bird in Santa's Beard

How a Christmas Legend Was Forever Changed

By

Jeffery L. Schatzer

with Mark Bush and Don Rutt

Illustrations by Ty Smith

The Big Belly Series

mitten press

Copyright © 2004 by Jeffery L. Schatzer

All rights reserved. No part of this book may be reproduced in any manner without the express written consent of the publisher, except in the case of brief excerpts in critical reviews or articles.

All inquiries should be addressed to:

Mitten Press
An imprint of Ann Arbor Media Group LLC
2500 S. State Street
Ann Arbor, MI 48104

Printed and bound in Canada

First edition 2004 Big Belly Books, revised edition 2005 Mitten Press
09   08   07   06   05   1   2   3   4   5

Library of Congress Cataloging-in-Publication Data

Schatzer, Jeffery L., 1949-
The Bird in Santa's Beard: How a Christmas Legend Was Forever Changed/ Jeffery L. Schatzer – 1st ed.
1. Christmas Story – Fiction.   2. Photography – Fiction

Library of Congress Control Number: 2004091312

ISBN-13: 978-1-58726-288-3
ISBN-10: 1-58726-288-6

To the wonder of belief

t happened the year that a cold, cold

winter had settled in the North. The birds

had long since flown to their warm nesting areas . . .

all the birds, that is, except one.

s Santa was on his way to look in on the reindeer, a squeaky little voice called to him. "S-S-S-Santa, I am f-f-f-f-freezing," a tiny bird chattered.

"Come, warm yourself in my beard," Santa said kindly.

Frup-frup-frup, the bird's wings flapped as it fluttered into the fluffy beard.

**T**rudging through the deep snow, Santa sheltered the bird from the bitter wind.

Upon returning home Santa made hot chocolate and oatmeal with cinnamon. When the bird poked its head out to look around, Santa asked, "Would you like some?"

The bird chirped in delight.

hey talked as they shared their warm meal.

The bird peeped about how much fun it is to fly high in the

sky. Santa agreed and spoke of how much fun it is to ride in his sleigh.

Suddenly, the bird became quiet and looked very, very sad. "What

shall I do? All the other birds have flown south, and I am all alone."

"Please stay with me," Santa said. And

that's exactly what happened.

Throughout the winter Santa and the bird became the best of friends. The bird even built a nest in Santa's beard. At bedtime Santa was careful to sleep with his beard and the bird outside of the covers. The bird didn't mind that Santa snored.

One December morning, Santa woke to loud

chirping sounds.

"Santa!" The bird flitted and fluttered with excitement.

"Wake up! Look and see! There are eggs in my nest."

Later that morning Santa whistled as he polished his big black boots. "Santa, you must be quiet and still," shushed the bird.

Suddenly Santa realized he had a big problem. "What shall I do? Every year before Christmas I visit with the children. Sometimes the children are noisy. Sometimes they wiggle around. I do not want to disturb your eggs, but I do not want to disappoint the children either."

I t was a big problem indeed.

Santa thought and thought. The bird thought and thought. They both thought and thought until their thinkers couldn't think any more. Suddenly the bird peeped and flapped her wings. "You have many grown-up friends. Perhaps they can dress to look like you and visit with the children. They can be your helpers!"

"What a wonderful idea!" said Santa. "Why, they can tell me who has been naughty and who has been nice. They can also let me know what the children would like for Christmas."

Together they talked to Santa's friends.

The grown-ups enjoyed dressing like Santa and visiting the children. The bird even helped by reading letters. Still, what was to be done about Christmas Eve? Santa just couldn't deliver toys with eggs in his beard.

n that magical night the bird chirped the answer softly into Santa's ear. "Though my eggs have not yet hatched, they are now strong enough to be moved. You must take my nest out of your beard. Please place us somewhere safe and warm. Then you can deliver toys to the children tonight."

anta smiled a big smile, and gently he combed

his fingers through his beard and lifted the nest.

Carefully he carried it over to the Christmas tree.

Softly he placed it on a sturdy branch.

ust before Santa flew off in his sleigh that night, the bird warbled a beautiful Christmas song. **Her music** was one of the most wonderful **Christmas** gifts Santa had ever received.

he eggs hatched the next morning. It was Christmas Day. Santa enjoyed the company of his bird guests that entire winter. In the spring the birds said goodbye and joined their friends. From time to time, the birds return for special visits with Santa.

Family reunion -
Last Christmas
Birds (left to right):
Maurice, Mama Clara,
Julius, Baby Ramona

o this very day, children often wonder why so many different grown-ups dress like Santa and help him at Christmastime. Now you know why.

It's because of the bird in Santa's beard.